AT
THE
POND

Geraldo Valério

GROUNDWOOD BOOKS
HOUSE OF ANANSI PRESS
TORONTO BERKELEY

Groundwood Books / House of Anansi Press
groundwoodbooks.com

We gratefully acknowledge for their financial support of our publishing
program the Canada Council for the Arts, the Ontario Arts Council
and the Government of Canada.

Canada Council   Conseil des Arts
for the Arts   du Canada

ONTARIO ARTS COUNCIL
CONSEIL DES ARTS DE L'ONTARIO
an Ontario government agency
un organisme du gouvernement de l'Ontario

With the participation of the Government of Canada
Avec la participation du gouvernement du Canada | Canadä

Library and Archives Canada Cataloguing in Publication

Title: At the pond / Geraldo Valério.
Names: Valério, Geraldo, author, illustrator.
Identifiers: Canadiana (print) 20190149051 | Canadiana (ebook)
20190159448 | ISBN 9781773062327 (hardcover) |
ISBN 9781773062334 (EPUB) | ISBN 9781773063621 (Kindle)
Classification: LCC PS8643.A422 A8 2020 | DDC jC813/.6—dc23

The illustrations were created with graphite pencil, color pencil,
acrylic paint, latex paint, color markers and a little bit of
gouache paint, on paper.
Design by Michael Solomon
Printed and bound in Malaysia

FSC
www.fsc.org

MIX
Paper from
responsible sources
FSC® C012700

to my friend Nilton

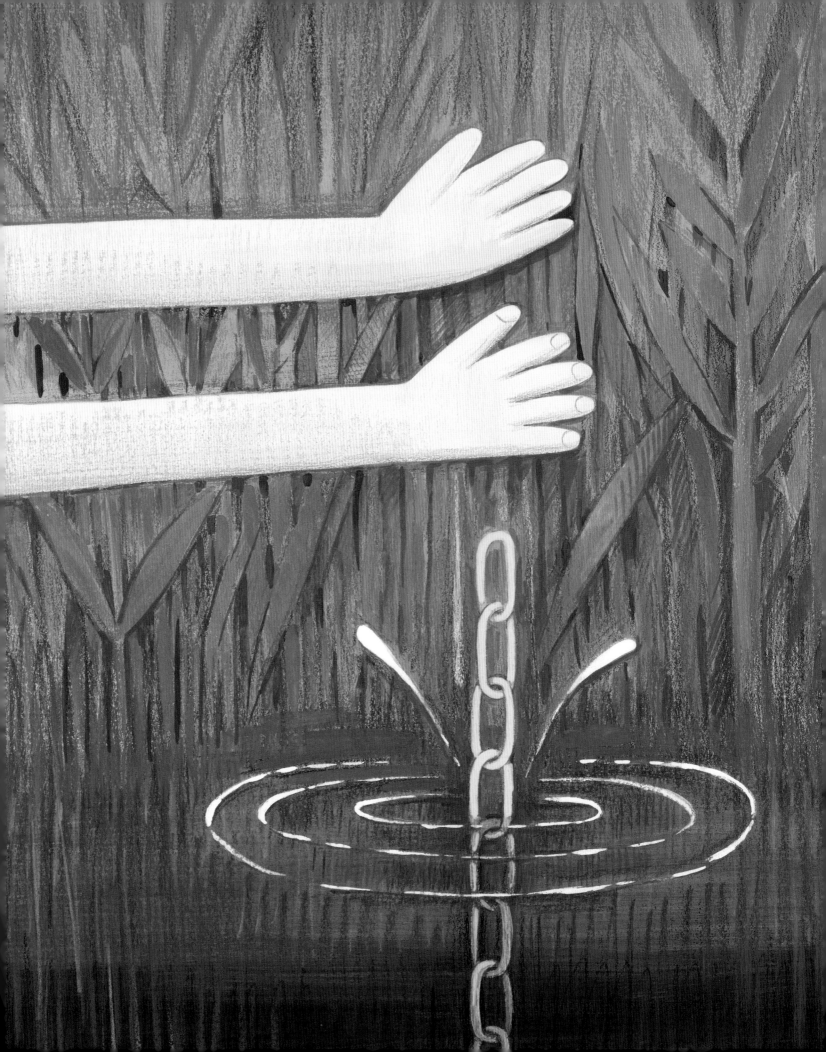